T0193476

COLLEGE TOOK MY SISSY AWAY!

Copyright © 2021 by Pamela, Kenady, Sydnie. 823696

All rights reserved. No part of this book may be reproduced or transmitted in any form or by any means, electronic or mechanical, including photocopying, recording, or by any information storage and retrieval system, without permission in writing from the copyright owner.

This is a work of fiction. Names, characters, places and incidents either are the product of the author's imagination or are used fictitiously, and any resemblance to any actual persons, living or dead, events, or locales is entirely coincidental.

To order additional copies of this book, contact:
Xlibris
844-714-8691
www.Xlibris.com
Orders@Xlibris.com

ISBN:	Softcover	978-1-6641-6445-1
	EBook	978-1-6641-6444-4

Print information available on the last page

Rev. date: 03/23/2021

COLLEGE TOOK MY SISSY AWAY!

Pamela, Kenady, Sydnie

UNIVERSITY
COLLEGE TOOK MY SISSY AWAY!

COLLEGE TOOK MY SISSY AWAY!
PAMELA SMITH, KENADY SMITH,
AND SYDNIE SMITH
ILLUSTRATION BY: TBD

Dear Reader,

My name is Kenady, but you can call me KJ. I'm 7 years old, and I have something to say…college took my sissy away!

UNIVERSITY

All my life, we were inseparable, but she's not here and that's unbearable!

When she went to college, I cried every day. College took my sissy away!!

Her clothes, her posters, her shoes are all gone.
Now I look forward to her calling on the phone.

But wait, there's good news I just thought about. I'm
the only child in the house and I have all the clout.

I get all the attention and that's so sweet! I'm the baby of the family and it's all about me!

No more sharing the bathroom, snacks or drinks. No more loud music when I'm trying to think.

This college thing is not so bad. Suddenly I no longer feel sad.

My parents are awesome, did I forget to mention?
While sissy is gone, I get ALL the attention.

Oh no! My sissy is coming home today. I hope she's not going to stay. College make my sissy go away!!

Thank goodness I finally got some peace. Until I get a visit from my baby cousin Elise.

Dedicated to Kenady and Sydnie for being the best daughters that a mother can ask for. Thank you for always supporting me and encouraging me to do what I love.

Printed in the United States
by Baker & Taylor Publisher Services